DEMONS IN THE DARKNESS

LessonsForLifeBooks.com

IMPRINT A Cross Man Comics Adventure

Demons in the
Darkness 4

© 2018 by
Keith M. Hammond
is published by
Lessons for Life Books, Inc.
St. Paul, MN 55116

ISBN 13: 978-1938588839. Printed in the U.S.A.

Cover design and layout by Keith M. Hammond.
Story concept and 3D Illustrations by Keith M. Hammond.
NOTE: Several software applications and 3D models and 3D props were used to create and generate and render the scenes and characters contained within this and other Cross Man Comics adventures. All are used by purchase or permission.

CROSSMAN
BOOKS

As **GENERAL DARKWING** flies toward the cavern where his team is now gathered, he begins to notice something very strange...

ARRIVING ON THE SCENE

DARKWING confirms that what he noticed flying in, is indeed what he saw.

3

As he settles into his vantage point across the cavern from the demonics, his suspicions are further confirmed...

and he falls...

...to the ground.

SUDDENLY...
the sky darkens and a portal opens up.

Lucifer and two demon dogs emerge.

AS THE DEMON DOGS
STAND GUARD...

Lucifer slowly comes into focus.

CAP grabs Satan's son in a chokehold.

He tells Lucifer that if he comes any further, his son is dead.

19

If you release my son now...I may let you live.

20

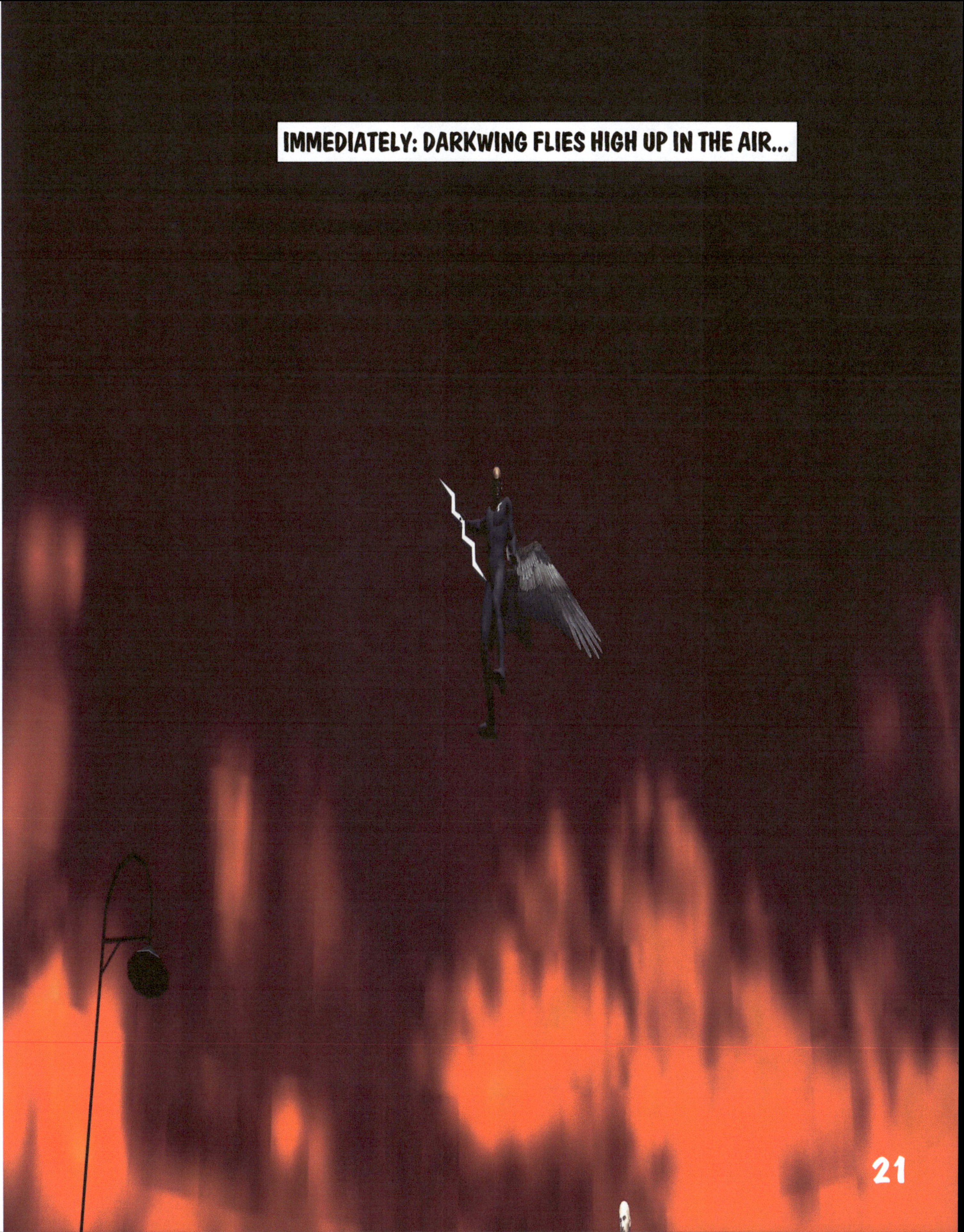
IMMEDIATELY: DARKWING FLIES HIGH UP IN THE AIR...

He tells Lucifer to back off, or he will use the Lightning Bolt, and they all will die.

Lucifer listens to DARKWING'S threat...
but responds: I will come back to get what it mine.

...and retreats back through the portal.

Lucifer's son is guarded by the team...

25

...who all know that this is a major victory.

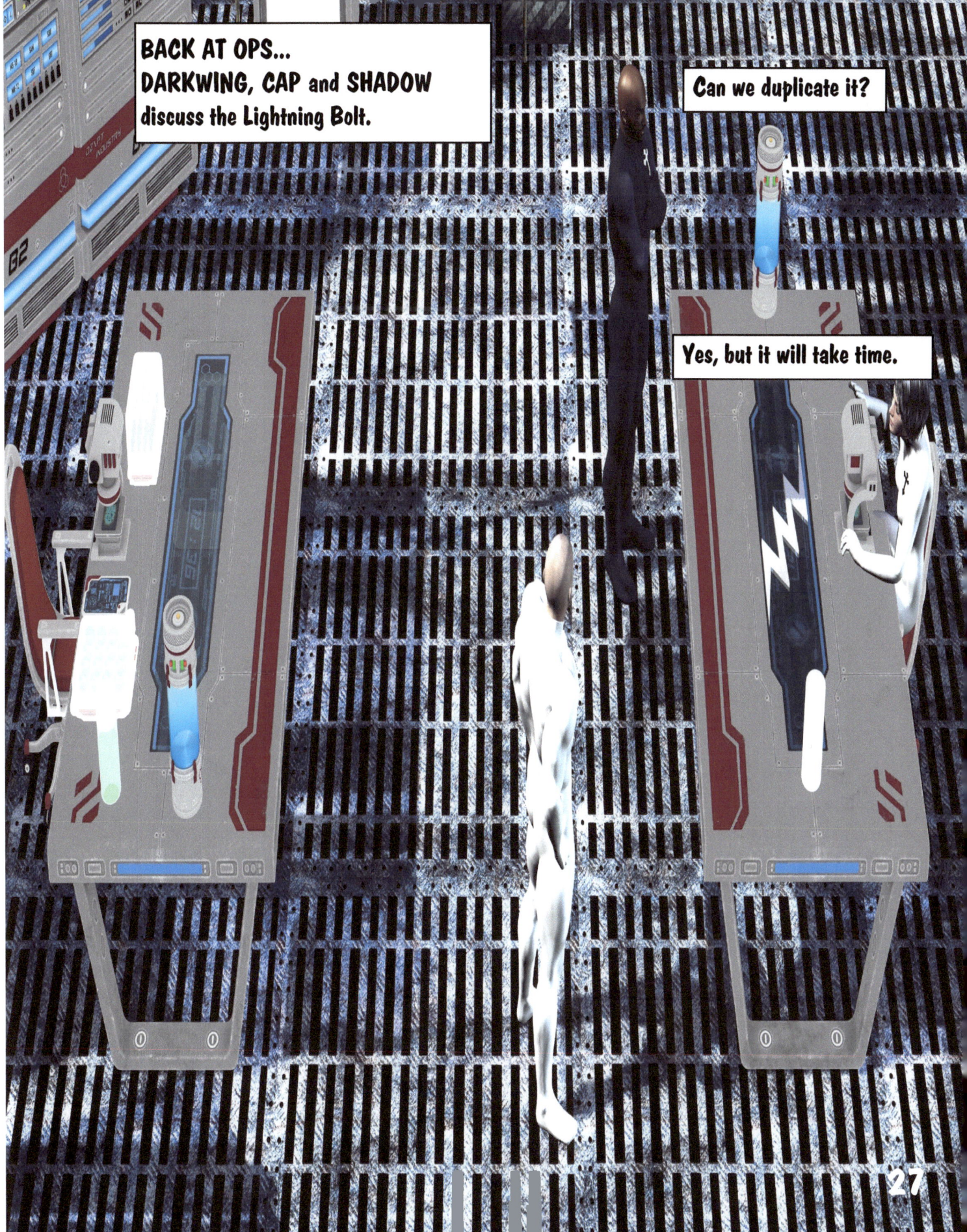

Time is something we don't have. Lucifer is not going to stay hidden for long. He is determined to get his son back any way he can. And when he says he will be back, he means it.

CAP, I need you to get in that lab and focus your efforts on finding out where they are hiding the rest of the Lightning Bolts.

As CAP heads toward the holding tank where Lucifer's son is being held, DARKWING tells CAP that he and SHADOW will join him shortly.

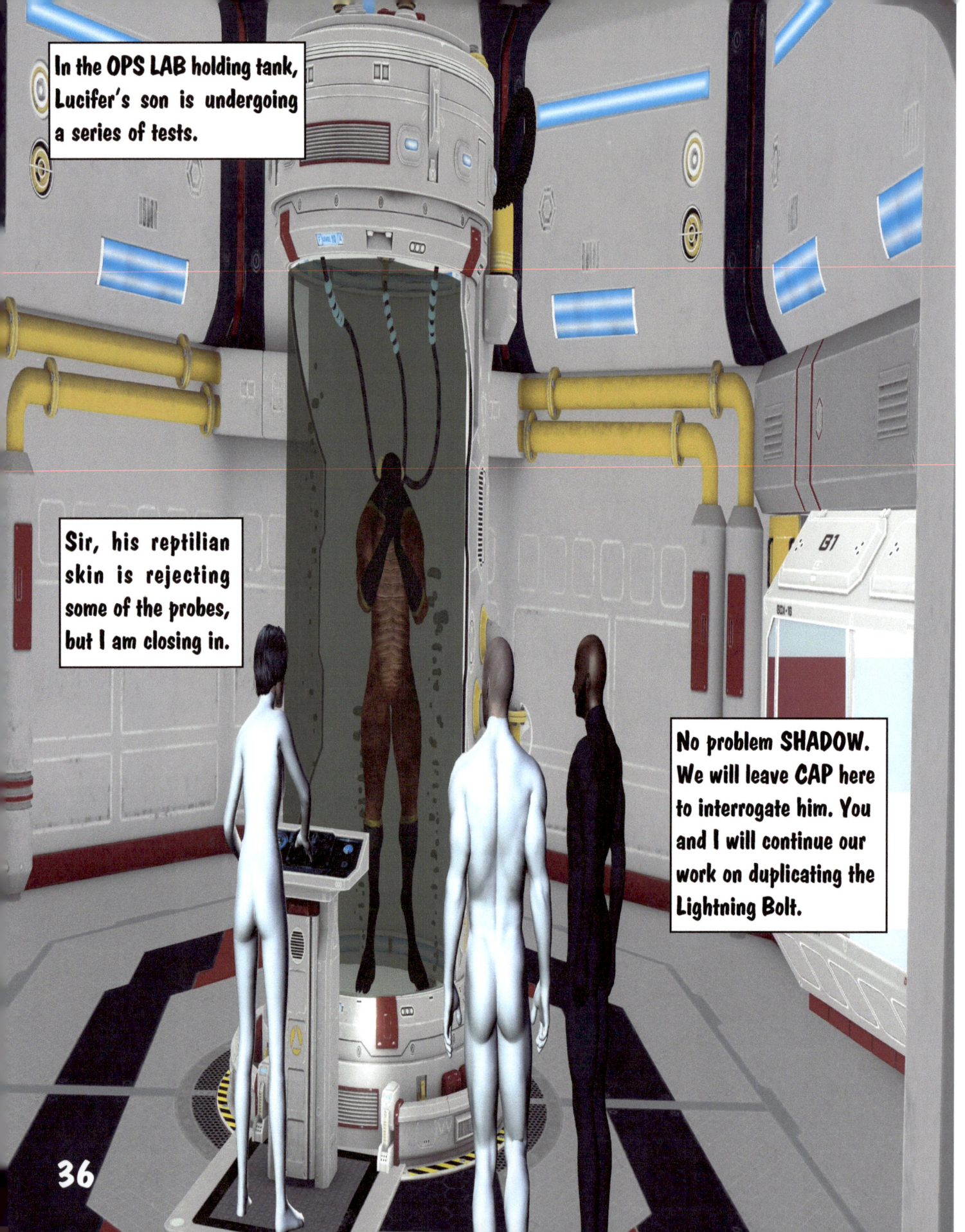

In the OPS LAB holding tank, Lucifer's son is undergoing a series of tests.

Sir, his reptilian skin is rejecting some of the probes, but I am closing in.

No problem SHADOW. We will leave CAP here to interrogate him. You and I will continue our work on duplicating the Lightning Bolt.

36

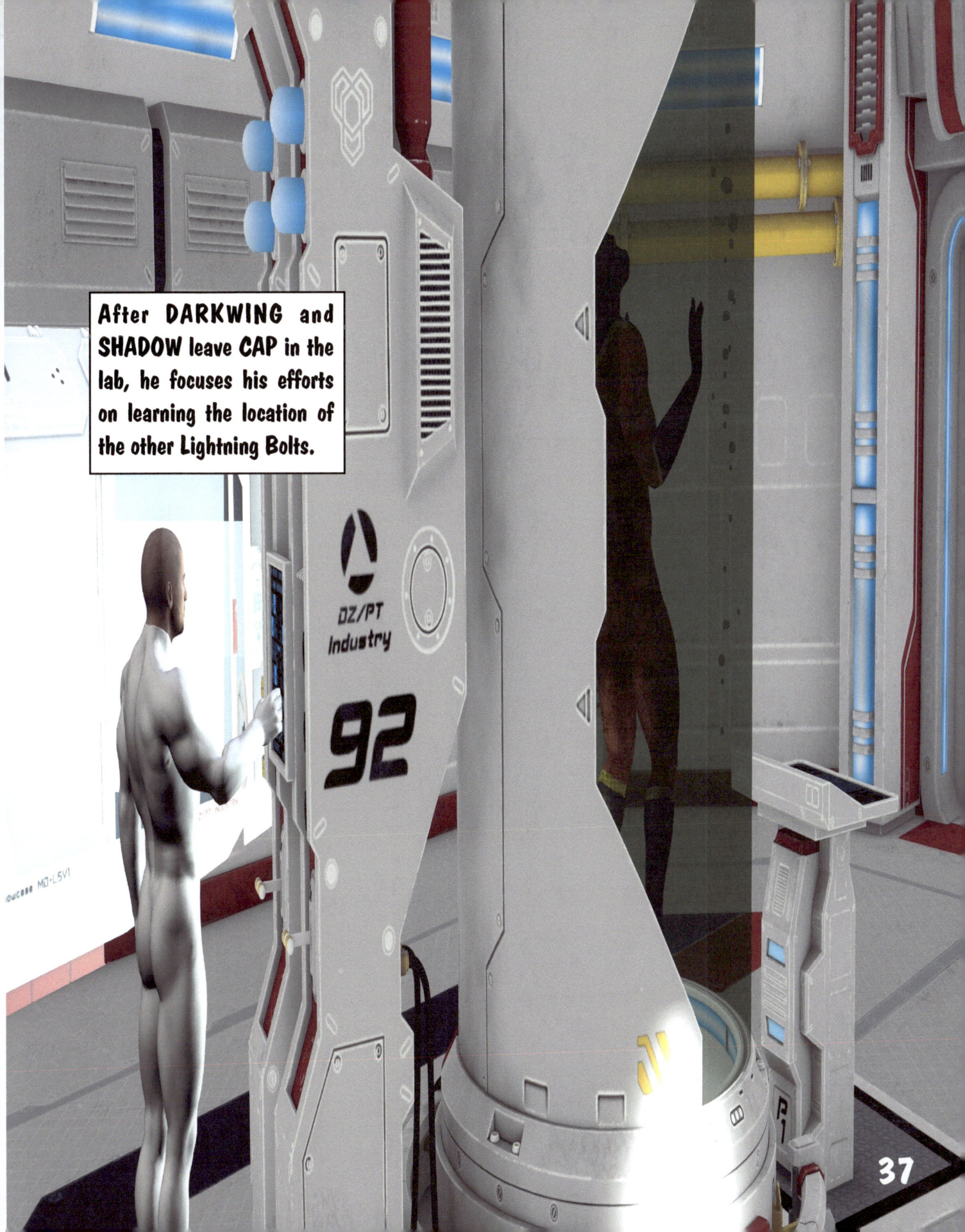

After **DARKWING** and **SHADOW** leave **CAP** in the lab, he focuses his efforts on learning the location of the other Lightning Bolts.

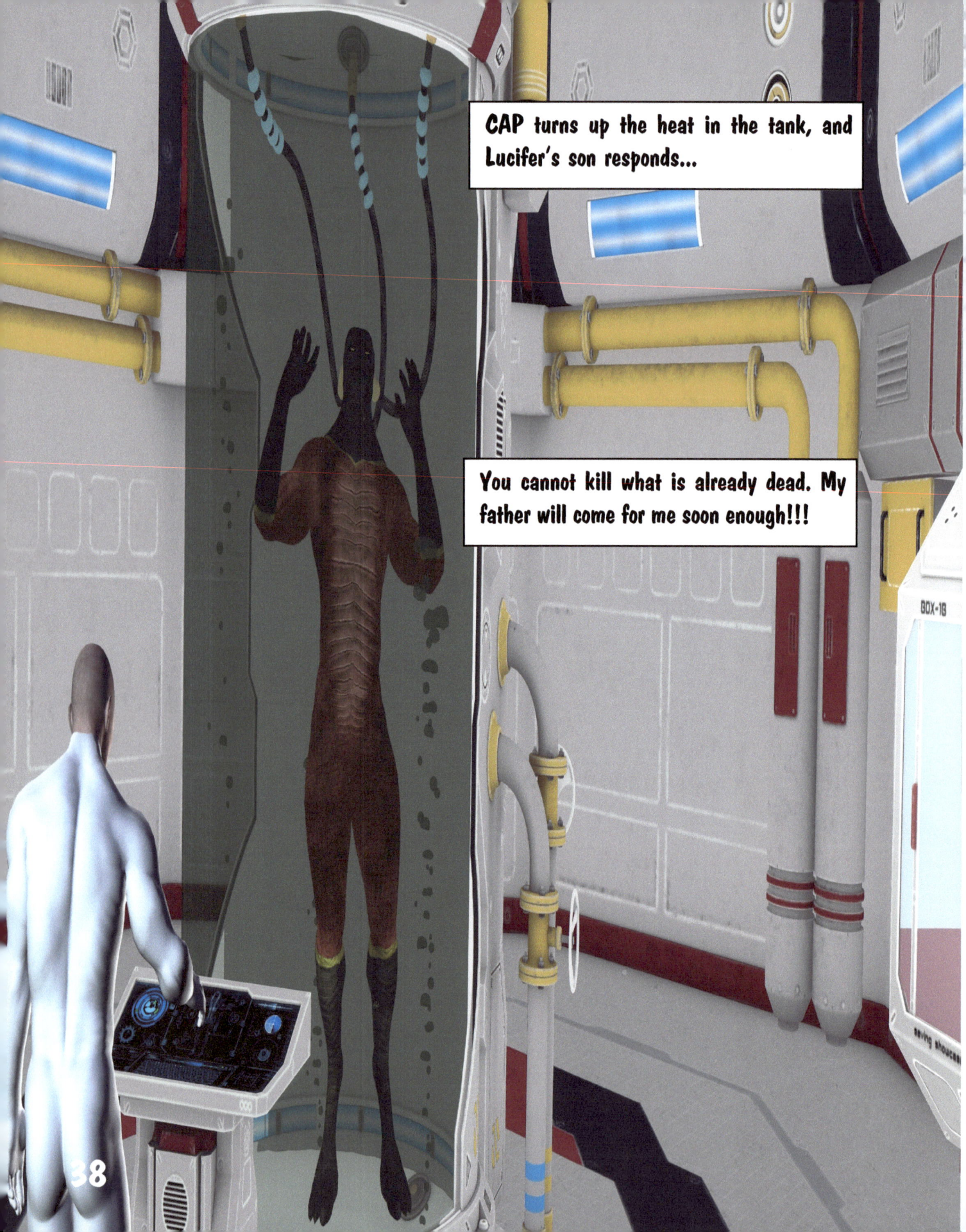

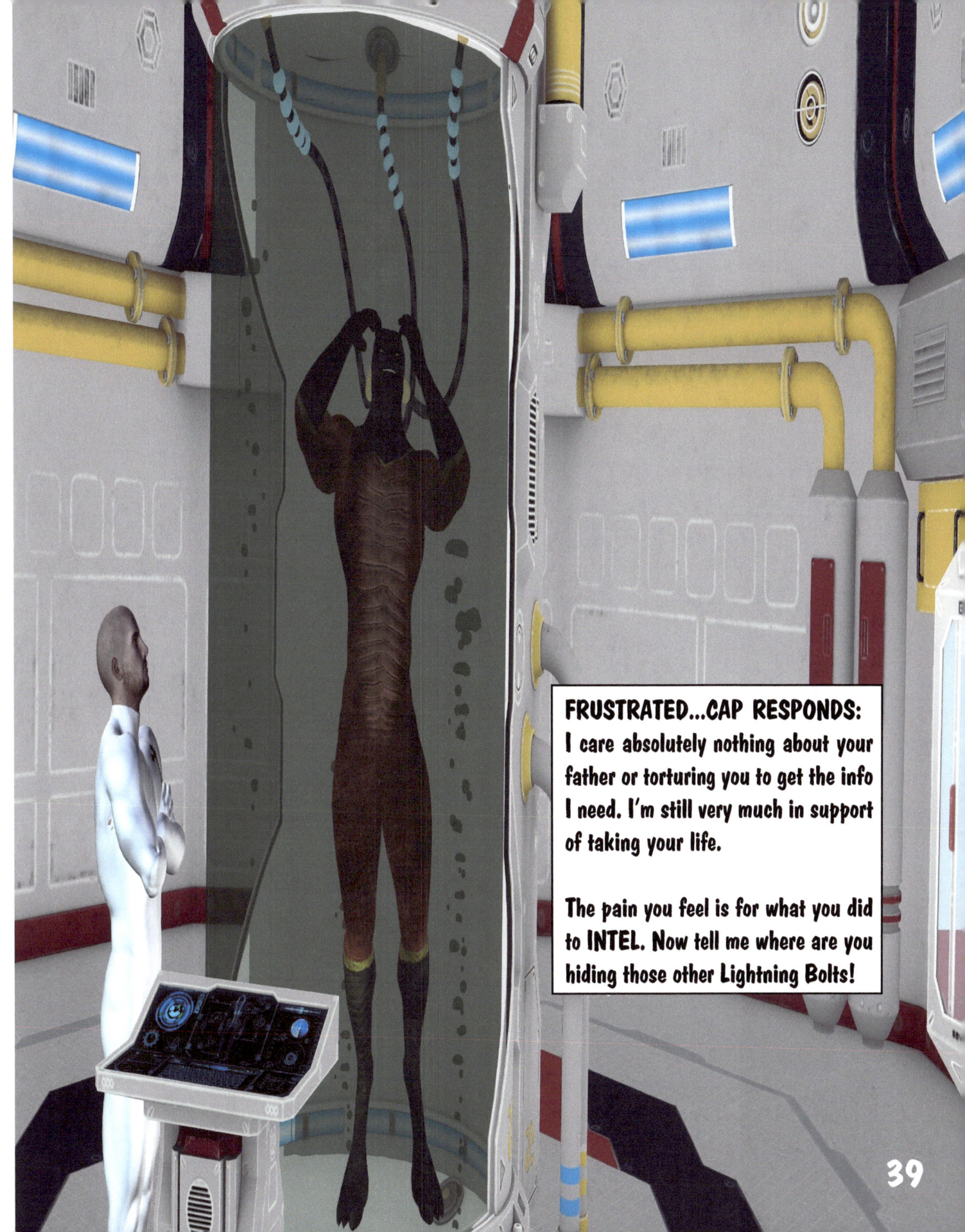

FRUSTRATED...CAP RESPONDS:
I care absolutely nothing about your father or torturing you to get the info I need. I'm still very much in support of taking your life.

The pain you feel is for what you did to INTEL. Now tell me where are you hiding those other Lightning Bolts!

GENERAL DARKWING calls the team together to brief them on the new weapons created from the Lightning Bolt formula.

This new arm cannon contains an electro pulse laser that can stun anything or anyone within a one block radius. Use it wisely.

We will use the devastation of the Lightning Bolt, if and only if there are no other options. These weapons should help us gain a lot of ground in this battle.

There are new mega lasers and stronger grenades; and the jetpacks and hovercycles now have weapon fire as well.

And, there are major differences between the old and new weapons, which you will be trained on when you are in the simulator.

43

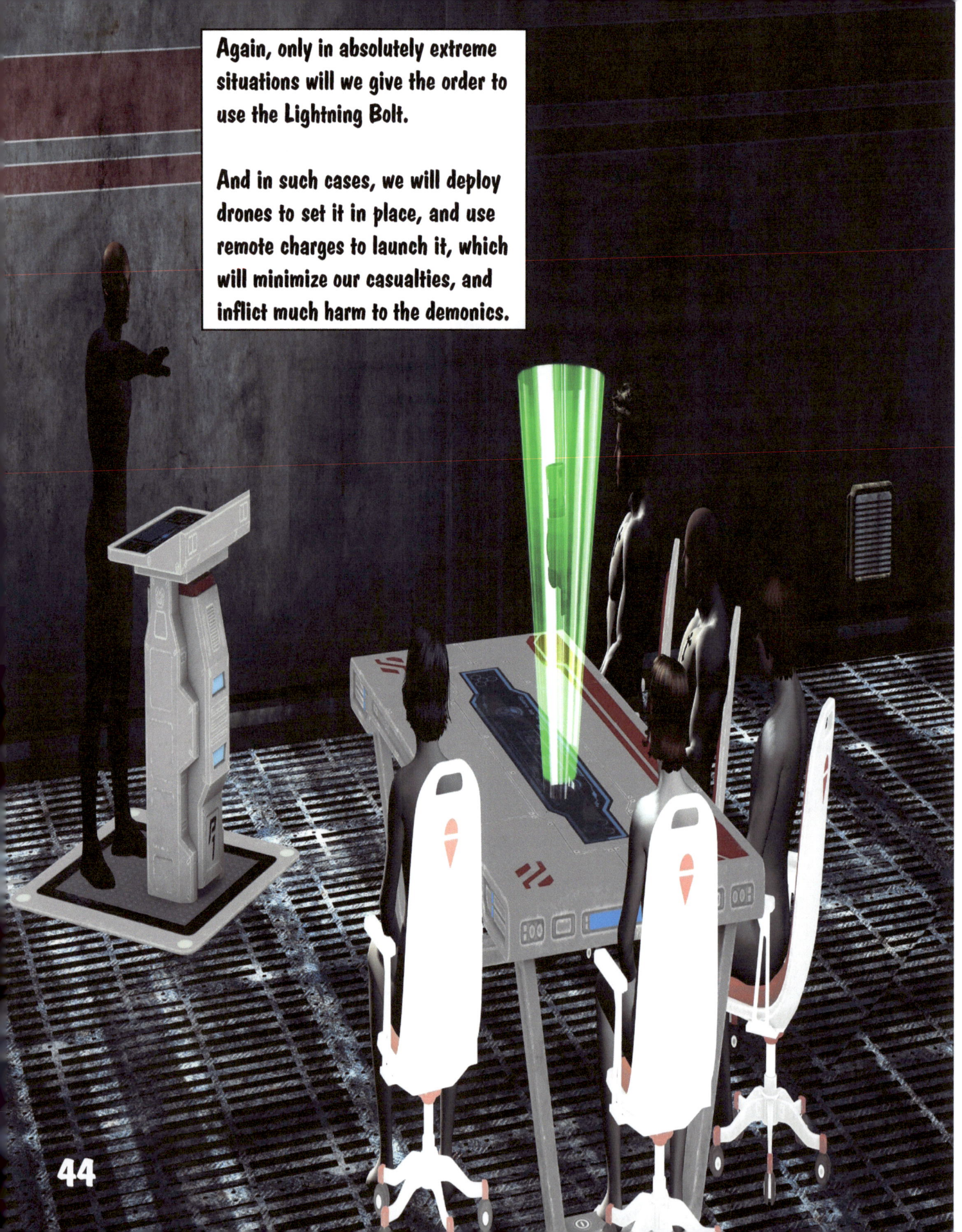

Again, only in absolutely extreme situations will we give the order to use the Lightning Bolt.

And in such cases, we will deploy drones to set it in place, and use remote charges to launch it, which will minimize our casualties, and inflict much harm to the demonics.

CIRCUIT enters the room and interrupts the weapons briefing. He tells the team that Lucifer's son has asked to be released in exchange for information on the location of a large cache of Lightning Bolts.

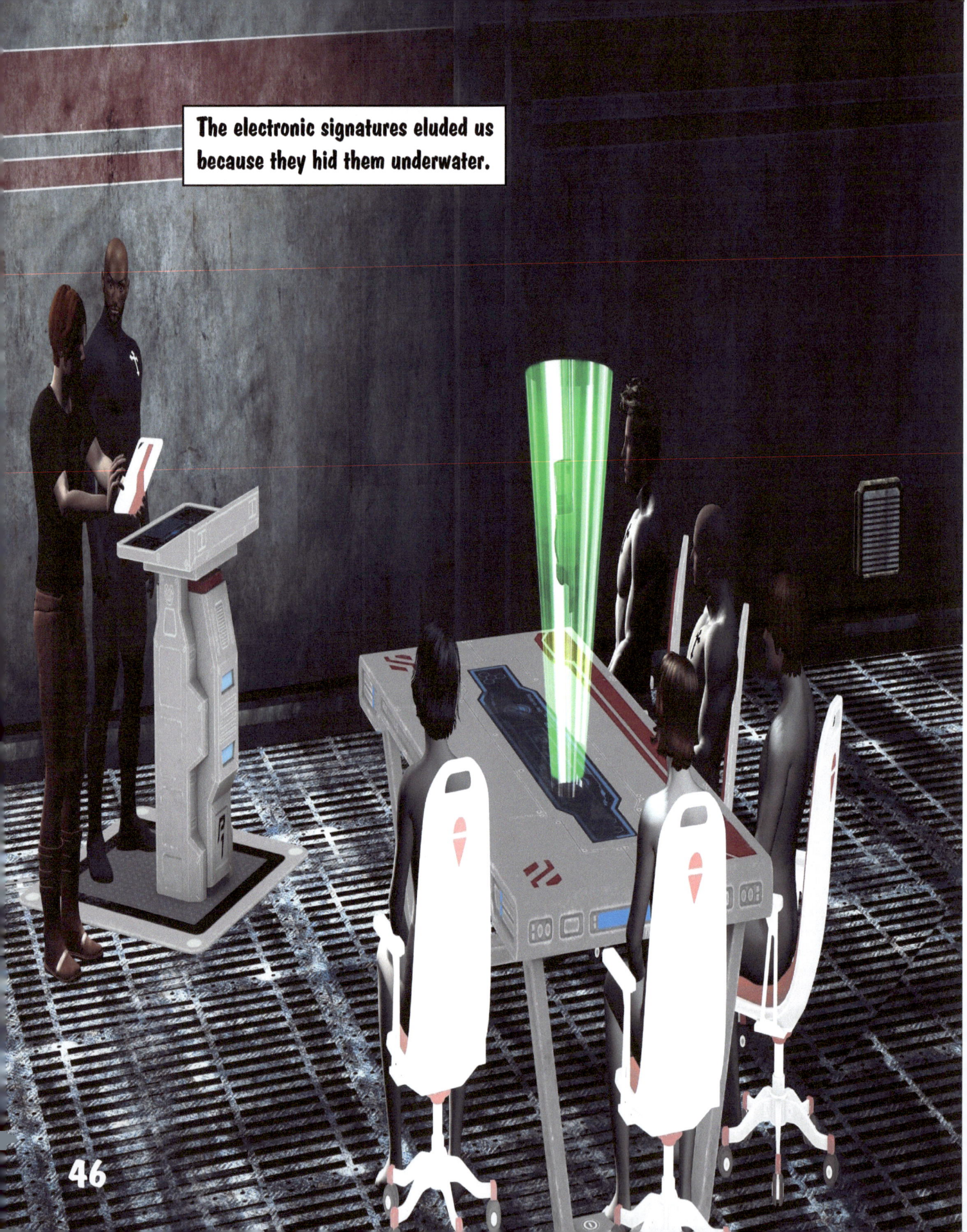

The electronic signatures eluded us because they hid them underwater.

At the first possible underwater location of Lightning Bolts, RANGERS arrive first, so they can assess the situation, and report...

They report their findings and prepare to take it down.

A sniper, posted high atop a mountain, reports seeing dragons in the courtyard.

Another sniper takes a spot inside a tower so he can lay down secondary fire in case the dragons take to the air.

And, so he can see anyone trying to escape from the rear or the courtyard.

HIGH ABOVE...

DARKWING, CAP and SHADOW fly in to take command.

53

STRENGTH is the first to engage, catching a dragon by surprise.

54

RANGER and RENEGADE fly in and flank.

FOX and INTEL approach from the East.

INSIDE THE CASTLE:

STRENGTH gives the team the all clear.

...then escorts CAP and DARKWING inside when they arrive.

STRENGTH reports that the team has secured the premises, and began their search for the other Lightning Bolts.

At that moment, SHADOW emerges from a room where the entrance to the abandoned well is located.

What could Lucifer be up to? Has he surfaced just to pick up his son? Get this answer and more in Book 5 of Demons in the Darkness!

And see videos clips from this book and the animated trailer for the upcoming film at... PastorKeith.org/trailer.

www.ingramcontent.com/pod-product-compliance
Lightning Source LLC
Chambersburg PA
CBHW041536240626

47164CB00002B/32